John J. St. Vincent

A Letter Addressed to the Gentlemen of England and Ireland

On the Inexpediency of a federal-union between the two kingdoms

John J. St. Vincent

A Letter Addressed to the Gentlemen of England and Ireland
On the Inexpediency of a federal-union between the two kingdoms

ISBN/EAN: 9783337184124

Printed in Europe, USA, Canada, Australia, Japan

Cover: Foto ©Andreas Hilbeck / pixelio.de

More available books at **www.hansebooks.com**

A

LETTER

ADDRESSED TO THE GENTLEMEN OF

ENGLAND AND IRELAND,

ON THE

INEXPEDIENCY

OF A

FEDERAL-UNION

BETWEEN THE

TWO KINGDOMS,

BY SIR JOHN J. W. JERVIS, BART.

Omne in Præcipiti vitium ftetit :   JUV.

All Crimes are at the Height !

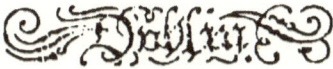

DUBLIN:

PRINTED BY JOHN WHITWORTH, 14, EXCHANGE
STREET.

1798.

GENTLEMEN,

THE prefent is a moft momentous Æra of the World.----It muft confti-tute a Period in the Annals of Time unequalled in antient or modern Hif-tory---almoft every Spot of the known Globe ftands involved in Scenes of mutilating Confufion, fevering human Confidence by Violence and Fraud, from the well-tried and eftablifhed Syftems of orderly Government; and fubftituting in their Room, the moft frantic Vifions of future Happinefs and independent Equality, founded upon the moft innovating Power of certain

A 2   coerfive

coerfive new-fangled Jurisdictions, whofe Judgments, as far as known to us, appear fubverfive of all regulated Order, and whofe Authority, being conftituted and eftablifhed upon the horrid Bafis of Plunder and Murder, refiftlefsly pervades through thofe ill-fated and unhappy Countries, who have fubmitted or fubjected themfelves to the Iron Yoke, with mercilefs and unceafing Fury, in the Extinction of all Religion, and the Wafte and utter Deftruction of all Property.

In this State of Things, whilft all are apprehenfive of the evil Confe-quences for a Time, at leaft, that are likely to enfue; yet there may be Room to hope that human Nature, being reftored to Reafon, we may be permitted to attend to the more mi-nute Matters in Society. Under this Hope,

Hope, I wifh to draw your Attention to a Subject of lefs extenfive Import- ance than that in which the civilized World is engaged, although nearly as portentous as any that ever attracted your Confideration; becaufe it is one that calls for your moft ferious Deli- beration.

The projected Union is the Subject I allude to :---May I call it a Phœno- menon, unexpected and of hideous Afpect.----In its Nature fo deftructive, that I would wifh, fondly to believe, even the prefent Times, fo creative of Novelty and Reproach, could not form or bring forth a more frightful Monfter. It is therefore ferioufly to be hoped, that the Report, though in general Cir- culation, is no other than the reftlefs Yearnings of a certain Tribe of mif- chievous Speculatifts, who range metho-
dically.

dically from Kingdom to Kingdom, for the fpecial Purpofe of deftroying Confidence, and deranging Society: And although I believe there can be no Ground for fuch circulated Report, yet, I deem it a Duty to fubmit my Ideas of the Meafure (if it is in real Contemplation) to your Judgment. Are we not fufficiently united? Are not the Interefts of both Kingdoms one and the fame, and depending on mutual Exertion?---The Report, therefore, cannot but be invented and promulged for iniquitous Purpofes as already mentioned; for it would be abfurd to imagine, that a Minifter who has fhown forth fo confpicuous for Ability and unwearied Perfeverance in an unexampled Struggle for the Honour and Happinefs of the Britifh Empire, againft the deftructive Principles inculcated by an indefatigable and inve-
terate

terate Foe, could for one **Moment,**
meditate upon fo pernicious a **Meafure,**
pregnant as it muft be, with every
Mifchief to the Realms of England and
Ireland!

You will be pleafed to obferve, that
fuppofing the Projection to be founded,
it is poffible the Event would be really
productive of far greater Mifchiefs to
the already almoft ruined Country of
Ireland, than in any Pofition it could
become to the nervous Syftem long
fince eftablifhed in England; becaufe,
in the firft Place, England having an
unrivalled Trade and Plantation Con-
nection, has it within her prefent Will
and Power, to reftrain and counter-
reftrain the ftrenuous Efforts of any
Rival-Nation, not connected with the
Meafures of her Finance or Government. As to her Situation and Influence,

ence, She is fo far fuperior in Strength
to her ill-fated Neighbour and neareft
Relative, that, although fhe is bound
down by every Tie of Blood and Af-
finity that can, or ever did fubfift
within diftinct Kingdoms, ftill in Con-
troverfion and Avoidance of obligatory '
Acts, does fhe manifeftly feek through
her legiflative Provifions, anxioufly to
claim a predominant Controul over the
flender Opportunities which, fhe has
afforded with fcanty Hand and needy
Diftribution to a grateful and affec-
tionate Sifter!

Why then fhall any ill-advifed Meafure be now judged expedient or neceffary to float itfelf upon the public
Mind, and to create Alarm and Doubt
to the brave, the generous and the
good, who have proved themfelves
ever ready to devote their Lives and
Fortunes

Fortunes in aid and Suftentation of the Prowefs of a Country already too much enriched through a Suction of Wealth from Pole to Pole!

My laft Queftion induces me further to ftate to your Confideration, that England, in point of her political Conftitution, being rendered perfect, or prefuming herfelf to be fo, would in all poffibility endure this innovating encroachment upon her fubfifting reprefentation, and Eftablifhment, with Apathy and Difmay, and of Confequence would not well endure or fubmit to an Intention, not only contrary to, but finally fubverfive of her legiflative Dignity: for prefently I fhall prove, that a well balanced Conftitution, fuch as fhe now enjoys, unequalled by any other, muft feel the Shock that would be occafioned through an Intro-

B   duction

duction of new Vifages, whofe palms being in ufage in the Realm of Ireland, might prowl about as Men in the dark, until difcovered by the Minifter's Wand of Surprize, whofe metalic touch reftores the blind to fight, as well as to other rapturous Feelings!

It is not fufficient to affert Facts, let us, from an extenfive view of what has happened, and is likely to happen, feek to form a Judgment upon the future.

Upon a late lamented Event, namely, the temporary Rebellion in Ireland, the Kingdom of England did nobly come forward, in Mind and Action, to the aid and relief of their fuffering brethren in Ireland.---Many of the Corps of that Militia, with peculiar and dignified Generofity, *Volunteered* their Services

vices to quell a Rebellion, the nature and inducement to which I shall not now trespafs upon you, in detail.----I am alfo perfuaded that fuppofing a like direful Event fhould happen in England, (which may Almighty God in his bountiful Mercy prevent,) the honeft Yeomanry of Ireland would, with un-daunted Courage, unanimoufly folicit the favor of Permiffion, to rufh for-ward to the difmay and defeat, of any foreign or domeftic Enemies in Great Britain.----I am then upon thofe true grounds, well warranted to pronounce, that, fuch a national reciprocity in Arms, and federal Action, conftitutes the moft beneficial Union, in fact and effect, be-tween the fifter Countries.

It might be ftrongly urged, as fully fufficient to Authorize fufpicion, of the fuppofed Projection, being in real agita-

tion,

tion, that it has not been yet difavow-
ed, by any Perfon empowered to
difavow it. Therefore the public
Alarm is hourly increafing in violent
Prefumption; whilft the feelings of
every Man, who yet remains in Pof-
feffion of a fixed Property in the
Country, are becoming more convulfed
through apprehenfion and real fear, that
the preponderating tokens of Vengeance,
hanging o'er his Head, will be realized,
through a decifion againft him, as
endlefs in its duration, as the Exiftence
of the Divinity, whom he awfully
adores!

I muft alfo obferve, that it becomes
incumbent and a Duty abfolutely neceffary upon thofe in Power, if
they are verily acquainted with fuch
Projection, to difclofe and make
known to you, who are the moft
interefted Parties, what the *Prologue*
of

of fo novel a Propofition entertains---
What are the Preliminaries---What are
the confolidating Truths----what are
the wonderful Inducements---who are
to have and retain the immediate Be-
nefits to refult from the iniquitous
Barter---who are the momentous No-
bility that offer to fupport it---who
are the Honourable Commoners who
wifh to exchange adverfe Situations
for temporary Quietude---what are to
become of public and private Credi-
tors---how is the capital City of Dublin to be preferved in her habitual
Rights---and finally, how are the in-
herent Rights of a great Nation, to be
preferved and handed down to Pof-
terity, undiminifhed and inviolate, as
we received them from the Hands of
our Anceftors?

Thefe Inquiries naturally lead us to
think it expedient, in order to form a
juft

juſt Opinion upon this momentous Sub-
jeƈt, that we ſhould be firſt acquainted
with the exaƈt Nature of the Meaſure in
ſuppoſed Contemplation---In ſhort, with
the *preciſe* Articles of Stipulation to be
finally adjuſted between the two Countries, as the Baſis of an Union ; and from
our becoming in that Manner acquainted
with the Minutiæ of the Meaſure, to
form our Opinions and Concluſions for
or againſt a Propoſition of that Mag-
nitude, which muſt conſequentially in-
volve the Happineſs or Miſery of future Generations!---But, I do ſay, that
although our becoming acquainted with
thoſe ſeveral Data, may ſeem abſo-
lutely neceſſary, yet it is to be ap-
prehended, that let whatever Stipulation be adjuſted in ſeeming Favour
to Ireland, ſtill it would be eaſy, at
any future Period, for a perverſe Miniſter to violate the Contraƈt as to
the

the weaker Country, in order to accomplish some wicked Measure, formed in Destruction of the Liberties or Revenues of both, or either Countries. Thus all the mighty Soundings of future Grandure and Freedom of Trade thrilling through our Ears, would vanish in Air; and therefore, such, or any Stipulation, be it ever so alluring, must be viewed by you as a delusive Fiction.

I do further say, if any such Scheme shall be proposed, that it may be safely laid down as a Fact not to be controverted, that the main object will appear to be, the absolute *Annihilation* of the Irish Legislature, thereby to enable an English Majority, acting under the Dictum of any corrupt Minister, to overwhelm the Revenues of this fated Nation, in an irredeemable

funded

funded Debt, notwithftanding fhe is already finking under a like Species of Incumbrance, brought upon her within the fhort Period of ten Years. The Meafure of a Union, be it pro-pofed when it may, cannot ever ori-ginate amongft, or come forward from, the real Friends of Ireland---It muft derive its Strength in the Coun-cils of a Britifh Cabinet. As that grand Object cannot be obtained otherwife than through an unbounded Influence over Ireland, it muft mani-feftly appear to the weakeft Under-ftanding, that, the *utter Extinguifhment of her parliamentary Jurisdiction*, will be the principal Aim and Object of Sti pulation; and in this Acquifition would all other fubordinate Confiderations in-ftantly merge. Here would end Ire-land's Security, and with it her Con-fequence!

Having

Having faid thus much upon a Subject, which I ftill flatter myfelf will
never be agitated, even by the moft
hardy; it may not, be either improper
or improvident, (leaft it fhould make
its Appearance,) to proceed in our
Examination of fo important a Queftion; and in order that we may come
as clofe as Prefumption will permit,
let us, for one Moment, turn our
Eyes to a Precedent, likely to be co-
pied as the Ground-work of a fimilar
Superftructure :----I mean the *Scotch
Union*.---Upon this Occafion, a few Reprefentatives of that Nation, were
transferred to the Britifh Senate ;---
and thus fhe loft her Legiflature!!!

In that Refpect, the Union with
Scotland would be literally followed, and
a Portion of the quondam Reprefentatives of Ireland (as they might then

c   be

be called) be *wafted* over to England, thus at once to repofe in the Hands of Englifhmen, equally ignorant and regardlefs of Ireland's Wants and Situation, an unlimited Power over her landed and monied Property :---This therefore, being the firft great Article that the Propofers of an Union would have in Contemplation, on it we may reft all the principal Mifchiefs that fuch a grievous Circumftance as the Deftruction of the Parliament of Ireland would be replete with to both Countries.---Who will tell me, that by the Death of the Parliament of Ireland, her Houfe of Lords and her Commons-Houfe, fhe would not lofe two of her Eftates out of three? Two of the integral Parts of her dearly valuable, and wonderfully nice Conftitution?---Her *Englifh Conftitution*-----*the Work of Ages!*-----

Her

Her *Legiſlature*, one Part of which holds the Balance between the Crown and the People, and maintains diſtributive Juſtice between Man and Man, as judges in the laſt Reſort, whilſt the other, through its vigilant Care, protects the Purſe of the Nation from the Attacks of every venal Miniſter. Deſtroy thoſe two Branches of her Conſtitution, and the beautiful Fabric is in Ruins!!

This Circumſtance, above all others, ariſing from this hated Meaſure, when duly conſidered, muſt particularly arreſt your Attention; for to preſerve this *great Barrier* of Society, the brave Yeomen of that Country did come forward with the laſt drop of their Blood, alike protecting every Branch of her conſtitution, as being all equally valuable and indiſpenſable---*Her King*---

Her

*Her Lords---and her Commons----*and mindful of their own perfonal Danger laſt of all!---Are they then to have this Barrier wreſted from them, after having vanquiſhed that defperate Party, who with *Lethal-intentions* to a matchlefs Conſtitution, dared to attack this *her Barrier,* for the Purpofe of overwhelming, in one common Deſtruction---*Her King---Her Lords---and her Commons!*---No Gentlemen, it cannot be; they have proved themfelves too deferving of its Protection.

Much however, as this Defpoliation would ruin the Conſtitution of Ireland, it would add nothing to the Profperity of England; nor would the Gentlemen of the latter Country, (as living under a fimilar Conſtitution to that which Ireland boaſts to enjoy,) wiſh to fee a People fo clofely connected

nected with them, as they are in every Refpect, deprived of that Barrier of Life and Property by which themfelves are protected!----Yet a UNION could not be without this Infringement!

Now behold the fad Train of Confequences, fuch a melancholy Circumftance would drag along with it. All who have their underftanding, muft perceive, at once, that when the few Reprefentatives of Ireland, would be *tranfported* to England, they would, either *naturally* or *artificially*, as being the *Minority*, fall into the *Majority*.--- It certainly would be in vain for them to attempt offering any Argument or reafoning againft the *will*, or, as it might be called, the *fixed Opinion* of Britifh Weight!---They could have no Influence againft fuch a *Majority*,

as

as would at all Times be brought forward, and would ever prevail in Matters of Opinion, as well as Intereft.----A Majority that would ever be for leaning hard upon *degraded Ireland*; for it is clear, that if any thing could induce thofe in Power at the Englifh fide of the Water, to wifh for the irrevocable Meafure of a UNION, of Legiflatures, between the two Coun-tries, it could only be with the Profpect of unjuftly obtaining Supplies, by draining Ireland, without having to call upon England.----Would it not be in the Power of a baneful Majority, headed by a fcheming Minifter, at any Time to demand a fubfidy from Ire-land, at the point of the Bayonet; when neither the fcheme would be approved of, nor Supplies to be obtain-ed from England?----It would be im-poffible upon fuch an Occafion, for

the

the few Reprefentatives of Ireland, (even though they were difpofed to act as one Man, in Support of the Rights of their Country,) to refift a Torrent that would carry every thing before it; notwithftanding a part of fuch Majority might even be compofed of Men who fhould be fo fhort fighted, not to fee it would be againft the future Intereft of England, to monopo-lize the poor earnings of Irifh Induftry, for the temporary Object of faving the Britifh Purfe.----Nor will it admit of a Queftion, that the fole view of the propofers of fuch a *provincializing* fyftem, would be to facilitate a road to Irifh Spoil, and thus to acquire a momentary Confequence, by fqueezing the Vitals of that Country.----And here we may add, that let what would be the Object of fuch a *ftripping Power*, and though it would be inconfiftent with found Policy,

by

by *crushing Ireland* in this Manner,
even the Britifh Empire would feverely
feel the Shock.---To tax Ireland would
become *the Order of the Day*---that abo-
minable Soil---that Country which the
Englifh have always been taught to
look at with diftafte, would not then
be fpared; nor is the Idea an unnatural
one, that Mankind being ever prone
to fhift the Burden off their own, upon
their Neighbours Shoulders, Ireland
though the weaker, would be made the
pack-mule on every Occafion.----Thus Ireland becoming deprived of her power
of Controul over her Finances, nothing
would remain to her of an admired
Conftitution, fave the *Executive* Branch;
in as much as the other Scale, together
with the Hand that poifes the Balance,
being cut off, her envied and Glorious
Bulwark of civil Society would crumble
away, and vanifh for ever!

Thus

Thus Gentlemen, would the Government of *both Kingdoms* become
completely abfolute, if it was not to
be dependent on the *Liberality* of the
People; for we may fay with De
Lolme * It is ftill from the Commons of England poffeffing this *powerful Weapon*, that the Monarchy is li-
mitted; but if the Government had
this uncurbed Power of obtaining Subfidies from Ireland, either by direct
or indirect Force, the boafted Check
would be for ever loft to both Nations, for Government would not have
to call upon the *Liberality* of the
People of England:---This would be
the Lofs of a Power which the fame
Author importantly defcribes, where
he thus expreffes himfelf---" The Right
" to grant Subfidies to the Crown,

(* Ch. 6. p. 74, 75.)

D   " poffeffed

" poffeffed by the People of Eng-
" land, is the Safe-guard of all their
" Liberties, religious and civil: It is
" a regular Means conferred on them
" by the Conftitution, of influencing
" the Motion of the Executive Power,
" and it forms the Tie by which the
" latter is bound to them." *---But a
UNION, by enabling the Minifter to
form any Majority he pleafed, or by
enabling him to exact Subfidies from
Ireland, would enable the Crown to
render itfelf independent on the Englifh Commons, in regard to its Supplies, by forming in this Way a Divifion, which would be the likelieft
Mode in the World of ftripping the
Englifh of this valuable Gem of their
Independence, or Appendage of their
Confequence, and is held forth by
De Lolme in the following Words:

(* Ch. 20. p. 513.)

(In

(in fpeaking of the Danger of the
People of England lofing this Privi-
lege by a Divifion of this Right,)
" Another Divifion of the Right of
" the People, much more likely to
" take place than thofe juft mentioned,
" might be fuch as might arife from
" Acquifitions of foreign Dominions,
" the Inhabitants of which fhould, in
" Time, claim and obtain a Right to
" treat directly with the Crown, and
" grant Supplies to it without the In-
" terference of the Britifh Legifla-
" ture." *

I have already ftated that the *nominated Reprefentatives* of Ireland would
be unable to ftem the Torrent of
Britifh Members, although they might
be inclined to do fo as one Man:---I
fhall go farther, and fay, that it is

(* Ch. 20. p. 522.)

moft

moſt certain that thoſe very Men, from the novel Situation they would find themſelves plunged in, would become ready and willing to betray and neglect the Truſt repoſed in them by their Conſtituents; their neceſſarily *long Abſence* from Ireland, would lead the Way to their forming new Alliances and new Intereſts; this, while it would render their new Reſidence attracting, would tend to efface from their Memories and Eſtimation, the true Intereſts of that Country they might ſuppoſitiouſly be preſumed to repreſent !---Thus would they ſoon come to be unmindful of the Charge repoſed in their Hands, notwithſtanding that a vigilant Diſcharge of their Duty in that Behalf, could be the only Return in their Power to make to their Country for confiding ſo important a Truſt to their Care:---But as they would have

their

their Seats *fecured for Life*, which would completely anfwer every Purpofe for them,---Indeed, as they could have no *real* Influence in the Britifh Houfe, it would be ridiculous for their Confti-tuents to trouble themfelves concern-ing them, for whatever Laws, urged by *Whim or Intereft*, Britifh Legiflation chofe to frame, could not be de-murred to. Hence even the Senti-ments of the moft loyal could have no Weight, either through the Repre-fentative or with him, for the Power of Election as well as all Check over the *nominated Member*, being pulled from the Hands of the Conftituent, but which has often-times proved to be beneficial, would be no more, and with it would go *the Wealth and Hap-pinefs* of the loyal People of Ireland---nor could that Applaufe which has ever followed a faithful Difcharge of

Duty,

Duty, as it then would be either un-
heard or unnoticed, be any longer a
Mode of rewarding Members for good
Conduct, as a powerful Incentive to
induce the Reprefentatives to adhere
to the Interefts of the Kingdom, in
Preference to Self-aggrandizement.---
Thus, it is evident, there would be
no Room to hope, while there would
be much Reafon to fear, that the Re-
prefentative would readily come to
overlook, and be regardlefs of his
Country's Welfare; nor is this all, for
it would naturally make the Way
eafy to ftill worfe Conduct---to ftu-
died Acts, diametrically oppofite to
their Country's Good,---and thus would
they readily fall into the crafty Defigns of a prodigal or profligate Minifter, (for however I may admire
the Englifh Conftitution, I cannot prefume that it is to make all Men
equally

equally juſt and wife,) that might unfortunately come to be at the Head of Affairs.---They would, in ſhort, become Inſtruments within the Reach of ſuch a Man, to aſſiſt in any dirty Work to be ſerved up as a *ſtanding Diſh* on all Occaſions, to the very great Diſcomfiture and Annoyance of the honeſt Engliſh Members, contrary to the Spirit of the Conſtitution of England, and the juſt Diſtribution of all its Parts, and thus no leſs injurious to the Privileges of Engliſhmen, than thoſe of Ireland.

But to take one more View of Scotland and her UNION, of which much has been attempted to be ſaid, by Way, I ſuppoſe, of anologiſtical Argument, although ſhe was differently ſituated both in Point of Territory and other adventitious Circumſtances, let

let us however dwell for a little on that fancied Model.

When we confider what was the real ftate of that Country, at, and long before her UNION with England, we muft fay there can be no Comparifon, nor fhould fhe be brought as a prece-dent now---She could not have been deemed an independant Country as Ireland, and indeed nature feemed to intend fhe fhould not.---Yet as to her Situation at this moment, what muft be faid?---Why, that of two Evils, though fhe may have chofen the leaft, territorially fituated as fhe is, She has no weight, nor could fhe carry any one point in the Legiflative Affembly of England, even though her Salvation was at Stake!---We muft therefore ad-mit, that nothing can compenfate for the Degradation fhe has fuffered by

her

her Union with, and Surrender of all her legiflative Rights to that Country, fave the *Peace* and *Quiet* fhe has fo *dearly* purchafed!

Circumftanced as Scotland was ter-ritorially, with a powerful Neighbour, whofe Armies having only to ftep acrofs the Tweed, that Country could never deem herfelf fecure from At-tack, had fhe not come under due Subordination by a Union, and with it, a Relinquifhment of all her im-portant Rights; fince which Period, although Edinburgh has extended its Limits beyond the Pale of a *confined Hill*, upon whofe Summit ftood her ftrong Fort and Watch-Tower, around which her crowded Inhabitants thought themfelves fafer than in the furround-ing Plane.----Yet nothing can, to my Underftanding, vindicate thofe (now

no more) who fuggefted and aided the
Scheme, fave the putting a Stop to
the perpetual Attacks that were to be
daily dreaded from her *Southern* Neighbours, thereby fecuring at leaft, the
peace and fafety of her People.----The
Advantages to be derived from peace
and quiet, were no doubt deemed,
(without having recourfe to bribes,) far
preferable to that State of predatory
Warfare, that to this Day, Scotland
might have been fubject to, had no
fuch Incorporation taken place.

This UNION therefore had a happy
Effect, in *conciliating* the two jarring
Kingdoms, and although the one loft
her Legiflature, yet from the Territorial
Contiguity of *both*, there is no great
Danger of the Parliament of England
dealing unfairly with Scotland, for the
Paffage of the Tweed, is as free to
the

the *now* Northern, as to the Southern Britons.---To keep Ireland down would however always be deemed neceffary, to make her yield to the frequent Burdens with which fhe would be loaded, not being fo eafy of accefs as Scotland; nor would there be any thing to fear from her croffing the Irifh Channel. Permit me now to obferve, that I have merely alluded to the *Scotch Union*, to fhew that her Legiflature, was upon that Occafion, merged in the Vortex of Englifh Power, and not to draw any inference therefrom, as, with Submiffion, I conceive the fame to be irrelevant to the prefent Queftion---but to return to Ireland.

Ireland is a Kingdom of no trifling extent, and prior to the late Rebellion, was advancing with rapid Strides towards Improvement, notwithftanding

the

the many Checks fhe had from time to time received, from the Jealoufy of her Sifter Kingdom, both in Manufacture and Commerce; and thus while fhe has been of immenfe Service to the latter, by the unlimited Importation, and Confumption of her various Productions, without having ever experienced any thing like Reciprocity.---What, therefore, muft fhe not expect to be faddled with, were fhe at the *fole Mercy* of her Elder Sifter?

Ireland divided as fhe is from England, can be fubject to no *inroads* from her Eaftern Neighbours.---They have by friendly Vifits, troubled her very little *indeed*---and confequently know nothing either of her State, or of her Wants.---Happy is it for her, and I truft for your Sake, and of the Britifh Empire, that fhe has her own diftinct Parliament,

Parliament, and a Parliament too, that has from time to time, framed for her moft wholefome Laws.----In fhort fhe cannot find it expedient or neceffary to furrender that Bulwark, of every thing that is great or good, for to purchafe fecurity from hoftile Inroads!

When Rebellion did raife its Hydra Head, againft the beft of Monarchs, and an envied Conftitution, (envied becaufe the nefarious find it a fhield againft conftructed Devaftation and Murder,) her gallant Sons, the Proprietors of her Soil and Wealth, with determined Loyalty, and undaunted Courage, came forward and crufhed it.---- They proffered their Blood, and their Treafure---for what? For the Protection of their King, their Country, and their Laws.----And are they now, as a

Reward

Reward for their Courage, and their Loyalty, to have thofe Laws furreptitioufly taken from them.

Thus did Ireland from her Activity and Spirit, call forth a Force, which without having recourfe to foreign Aid, was fufficient to curb the many headed Traitor.---Nor had fhe been backward within the Walls of Parliament in voting, and without its Doors, in fubfcribing pecuniary Aid, during this unparralleled War of Aggreffion, on the part of a frantic Foe, for the purpofe of repelling his feveral Attacks.

After this Digreffion, allow me once more to turn your Attention to the main point in Queftion, and afk whether the Annihilation of the Irifh Parliament, as already defcribed, would not be a fufficient proof of the *ruinous* tendency of a UNION between the two Coun-

tries,

tries, without which it could not be.---
Here lies the Bane of the Meafure;
for with whatever glare of colouring,
the Propofition may be blazoned, ftill,
" *Latet Anginis fub Herba,*" and any bar-
gain that might be made, as to a right
of Reprefentation, be confidered as a
mere Delufion.

Permit me, Gentlemen, to go ftill
farther, and fay, it would be better for
Ireland, could fhe make fuch furrender
of her Privileges, to pretend to no right
of Reprefentation whatever, as, in that
Cafe no *vain* Expectations could induce
honeft Men to venture their Capitals,
in uncertain undertakings; and thofe
who might otherwife be the *quondam
Reprefentatives,* with their followers,
would ftay at home, and by their Money
and their Prefence, encourage the Cul-
tivation of her Lands; for, under the

fpecious

specious Appearance of Representation, she would have none in fact. If the Kingdom could be viewed, on that Occasion, even as Scotland, or be as certain of Security as Yorkshire, then we might consider the paucity of Representatives, a Matter of no great moment; but as a UNION can be desired for no other Purpose, than to put the Minister above the *Liberality* even of the *English Commons*, a strong Party in that House, independant of the Irish Members, inclined to shield Ireland, would be the only means of Security.---This however is not to be expected, for as it is to obtain a *Party* independant of the English Members, that, the Acquisition of Irish Force is sought for, so they would with some others become the very Persons paramount to the faithful Commons of England, as alluded to in the following Words

Words by De Lolme---" If any other
" Perfons befide the Reprefentatives of
" the People, had a right to make an
" offer of the Produce of the Labour of
" the People, the Executive Power
" would foon have forgot that it only
" exifts for the Advantage of the Pub-
" lic." *

While thus it is manifeft, that both
Countries muft be led to the brink of
Ruin, by fuch a Debafement of *public Rights,* it cannot but appear alfo
that both would fuffer extremely by the
private Rights of the People of Ireland,
now fully protected by her Houfe of
Lords, as *Judges* in *the laft refort,* coming to be finally decided upon by the
Englifh Houfe of Peers, whither her
appellant Jurifdiction, along with a
few of the Members of her Supreme

* Chap. 8. p. 85.

F   Judicature,

Judicature, would be moved to.----I particularly allude to the Right of Property.

This Inconvenience would give a fevere blow, indeed, to her Hopes of further Improvement.----No Man could be fure of a fair Inveftigation of his juft Claims. Hence I may afk would not this materially check her Progrefs in Commerce and Manufactures, if not, totally deftroy all Attempt that way?---- Would not this be a neceffary Confequence from the belief that private Property was no longer fecure?

In this way one of the principal *private* Rights of Individuals being *Property*, would come to be in a very precarious State truly, independant of the Attacks on it in the way of Taxation. If England has flourifhed from the very

Reverie,

Reverſe, each Individual being ſen-
ſible of his excluſive Right to enjoy the various Fruits of his Induſtry,
why ſhould Ireland proſper without
this Security? *Quod Rectum, rectum eſt* ---
may be the Anſwer of ſome, but in
order that any ſhould impreſs you,
Gentlemen, with the Idea that a great
Miſchief would not follow ſuch an
Innovation in the Upper Houſe, *the
Judges of Ireland in the laſt reſort!* ---
let them in denying my Poſition prove
their premiſes. But I ſay, by this
would be loſt the Check, which, the
Individual now has a Power of bring-
ing againſt the corrupt Deciſions of
any future Judges, who may come
to preſide in our inferior Courts; for
while the Remedy would come to appear uncertain, the Search after it
would be worſe than the Diſeaſe. --
The *Levity* of Judges, when convinced

that

that there was no effectual Mode of doing away their light Decifions, might very likely become frequent; for, although Man, when properly curbed, becomes a very rational, honeft and harmlecfs Animal, yet if not chained down to fome Rule of right Reafon, may be expected to become quite the reverfe: and though the Judges of the Land are, under the prefent Conftitution, a very upright Body of Men, and *deliberate* in Decifion; yet it is to be feared, that when the Reftraint was removed, a Departure from fuch neceffary and Praife-worthy Conduct might in Time creep forward into Ufage, to the irreparable Injury of thofe feeking an impartial Diftribution of Juftice; nor has this Dereliction of Juftice been unfrequent in the World.

De Lolme.

De Lolme, in fpeaking of the Judges of antient Rome, adds thus---" Nor " were the Roman Magiftrates fatis- " fied with committing Acts of In- " juftice in their political Capacity, " and for the Support of that Body " of which they made a Part: Ava- " rice and private Rapine were at " laft added to political Ambition."*

On a Deprivation of the Irifh Judges Right to fit in Parliament, there may be Room to prefume, that the Lofs of the political Influ- ence which they now bear, muft be compenfated for, in fome other Re- fpect.---It has been deemed, that the Increafe of their Salaries, and the Te- nure under their Patents being en- larged to a Term for Life, have con-

*Chap. 16. p. 350.

ftituted

ftituted a fufficient Security for their
ftrictly attending to a due Adminis-
tration of Juftice; but as the Provi-
fion fhould be to guard againft the
worft poffible Cafe that might occur, every Care fhould be taken to
prevent future Mifchiefs. The Irifh
Houfe of Peers having recovered its
Appellant Jurisdiction, uninfluenced by
any other Body, whilft it is deeply
interefted in the Property of the
Kingdom, and being the *fupreme Court*
of Judicature, provides this Remedy:
But *è contra*, if a few of the Members
of that Houfe became immerged within the Controul of a more numerous
Body not fo much interefted in the
Property of Ireland, and therefrom liable to be led aftray in their Decifions---where then would be the Remedy?

Here

Here I would fubjoin one Remark---
That, although the Example of Scotland has been fo much relied on, it
cannot, in this Place, be pawned
upon you;---For the Laws of Scotland
differ fo much from thofe of England,
that the Judges of the latter, much
lefs the Peers, can pretend to no Controul over the Peers of the former;
and, therefore, the Peers of Scotland
become the *real* Judges on *Appeal*.
But the fame Obfervation cannot hold
as to Ireland, for the Englifh Peers
would, from the Similarity of Englifh and Irifh Laws, be always deemed
competent Judges to decide on Quef-
tions touching *private* Property in Ireland, and therefore the Peers from Ireland become, at leaft, indirect Coun-
tenancers of *Injuftice*.

In

In this Manner the *Affurances* of the Realm would become ufelefs, and the Effects form a Parallel to the Tres-paffes defcribed by De Lolme as touching Roman Judges at a certain Period, in the following Words:---" The " Laws and public Judgments not only " thus failed of the End for which " they had been eftablifhed: They " even became, at length, new Means " of Oppreffion added to thofe which " already exifted. Citizens poffeffed " of Wealth, Perfons obnoxious to par-" ticular Bodies, or the few Magis-" trates who attempted to ftem the " Torrent of the general Corruption, " were accufed and condemned:" *---In this Way the Properties of Individuals might come to be at the Mercy of *Avarice* or *Caprice*, and well-

* Chap. 16. p. 353.

framed

framed Laws be rendered of no avail.----Here, I am convinced, you will exclaim after the Manner of the ancient Englifh Barons---" *Nolumus le-* " *ges Hiberniæ mutari!*"

As the upper Houfe of Parliament in that Country now ftands, we may ftill dwell on De Lolme, and fay with him---" In the Exercife of their ju- " dicial Authority, with regard to ci- " vil Matters, the Lords have mani- " fefted a Spirit of Equity, no wife " inferior to that which they have " fhewn in their legifiative Capacity. " They have in Difcharge of that " Funɛtion (which of all others is fo " liable to create Temptation) fhewn " an Uncorruptnefs really fuperior to " what any *judicial* Affembly in any " other Nation can boaft, nor do I " think that I run any Rifk of be-

G " ing

" ing contradicted, when I say that
" the Conduct of the House of Lords
" in their civil judicial Capacity, has
" constantly been such as has kept
" them above the Reach of even Sus-
" picion or Slander." *

But on a Surrender of her Peers,
Ireland could not make this Boast,
for it is next to a certainty that no
Cause would be fairly decided; be-
side the Expense would render the
Reference to the supreme Jurisdiction
in England, (by which to obtain final
Justice, if thus it could be arrived at)
a thing almost unattainable.——Thus
this great *Sanctuary* against the Caprice of a single Judge would be for
ever lost.

You certainly will allow there is nothing more indispensably necessary for

(* Chap. 16. p. 374.)

the

the well being of Society, nor any Thing more productive of Improvement in a Country, than that the Property of Individuals should be thought *secure;* but to this End justice should be administered with an *equal Hand,* as also be dispensed at an *easy Rate.*----So different an Effect would such an UNION have, as involving a Loss of the upper House of the Irish Parliament, that, you will readily admit the Decision of Causes on Appeal would be very *partial*---It would at least be very *Expensive!*

From hence Gentlemen you must see that on a UNION, the *Public* and *Private* Rights of Ireland, would in every Respect be at the Mercy and disposal of a Party---A Power I am conscious the Friends to either Country could not wish to see created, as both Coun-

tries

tries would have to dread the Confequence.

Having faid thus much as to the Effect of thofe political Innovations, I muft add another Proof of the Injury the two Kingdoms would Experience from the Annihilation of the Irifh Legiflature---but at the fame Time I muft allow, that what I am about to ftate, although of immenfe Importance, is as well as many other Points of a fubordinate kind, compared to the foregoing; I mean the Deftruction of that *Spur*, to Exertion and Induftry by which alone, Commerce and Manufactures, (the Sources of the Wealth of Nations) are brought to Perfection; and this by leffening that Appetite for Diftinction, which Men may now arrive at, by acquiring a Seat amongft the Reprefentatives of the People.---It is at prefent,

in

in both Countries, an incentive to use-
ful Activity, and operates forcibly in pro-
moting important Refearches through
literary Improvement.

But upon new modelling the Conftitution in the Manner pointed out, none
who are confined to *active* or *ufeful* Em-
ployments, could be among the Num-
ber of the *chofen-few*---Thefe could not
fpare to fpend a Year in London---the
Prefence of the great *Manufacturers*,
Merchants, and *Lawyers*, is neceffary
at home---Thus all thofe muft be ex-
cluded, and of courfe deprived of a
favorite Object, which, otherwife would
ferve as a Reward for their Affiduity
and Labour.---I am fure, you Gentlemen, cannot relifh fo new fangled an
Experiment!---The Gentlemen of Ireland cannot, and *Fellow-feeling* at leaft
forbids thofe of England---confcious that
they,

they, themfelves, could not endure to be deprived of fuch a *Right:*---I muft here afk, whether it be not a thirft after Diftinction and Fame, implanted within the Breaft of Man, that roufes him to thofe Exertions which tend to the Improvement of the Arts?---I do believe that this defire Operates more univerfally and forcibly, than the fordid Idea of hoarding up in Coffers, which latter, we find a very rare thing. If then this very praife-worthy Ambition is clogged, the progrefs towards Improvement in the ufeful Arts is checked; and I do believe, that Man in fuch a State of Things, would have no other Idea, than to merely exift. On the contrary, why does the Merchant or Lawyer, labour for the greateft Part of a Life, but to arrive at Diftinction, by being honoured with a Seat amongft the Reprefentatives of the Feople.

People.---Hence this may be efteemed a very great Spur to Commerce and the Arts---but take away this *Stimulus*, and you deftroy the energetic Spirit; nor would Ireland alone fuffer by this; for her confequent Decreafe in Wealth would be feverely felt by England, as the latter muft ever acquire additional Weight in the Scale of Europe, from the increafed Wealth of the former;--- a fevere blow this, to the future Confequence of Great Britain, notwithftanding the temporary Benefit it might be fancied to derive, from a Minifter being able to raife the Sums he wanted off Ireland, without having to apply to the *Liberality* of the Parliament of either Country.---It is true England would no longer have to dread Ireland becoming her Rival in Commerce and Manufactures, but fhe would have to lament the want of her very powerful

Support

Support as an Ally in Time of War, and of her Imports in Time of Peace.

I have Gentlemen, fubmitted for your Confideration, the *horrid Idea* I entertain of the Meafure of fuch a UNION, as affecting *both* Countries.---- It now only remains to point your Attention, moft particularly, to one very important Confequence immediately affecting England, but which would in the End fpread its baneful Effects, to all thofe Countries and People, that are under her Sovereign Power---I mean neither more nor lefs, than the *total* and *radical* Deftruction of her *Glorious Conftitution!*---This would be a lofs which would reduce her People, and every Thing along with them, to a ftate equally degraded as Ireland--- Their right of granting or withholding Supplies would be alike defpifed, for

on

on fuch a UNION taking Place, *Ireland* would be at all Calls bound to fupply the Demands of the Minister; and thus the *Power* of the *Crown* would be raifed to an unexampled Pitch, at once deftructive of the *Balance* of the Conftitution, and the noble Fabric it-felf!---Confider the Danger of fuch an *extenfive* Power in the Hands of a Mi-nifter, and alfo how feldom fuch an unknown Power has been wifely direct-ed.---You will readily behold, in this Acquifition of *minifterial* Influence, the *lofs* of that moft valuable Part of your *Bill* of *Rights*, which gives to the Peo-ple of England, a *full Power* of curbing the *Exploits* of a Minifter, by a *refufal* of the Means to carry them on, and finally an Eftablifhment of abfolute Sway.

What

What might not be the fatal Confequence of a pernicious Direction of this increafed Power, it is impoffible to fay----furely a Country like England whofe *proud Elevation* amongft other Nations, has grown out of a *well poifed* Conftitution, could not relifh a Scheme of this Kind! We have had a fad Example before us of the fatal Confequences of Defpotifm.----In France we have beheld all the Miferies of a Civil War----The *People* of *England* have heard enough of the fad Difafters, which have followed a *too diftended* Power of the *Crown* under a *Steuart*.----And they have learned from their Anceftors, the Neceffity of holding the *Purfe of the Nation!*----A Power that would no longer remain, was the Wealth of Ireland to be fquandered away at the Pleafure of any Minifter.

How

How many even in the prefent State of Affairs, have found fault, with the increafing Power of the Minifter---The late and prefent Times certainly juftify much energy---But although all were now moft fully to agree, that the feveral Branches of the Britifh Conftitution *are now well balanced*, you cannot however hefitate declaring that a UNION with Ireland, on the foregoing *Broad-bafis* would moft certainly *deftroy* that Balance, and that the Power of the *Executive Branch* would *then* be too great.

In favour of the Meafure as to Ireland, it has been vainly held out, that Englifh Capital would flow into the Country---Irifh Capital would flow out of the Country in every Shape, and daily diminifh with declining Induftry. It feems extremely abfurd to think,

that

that Englifhmen would leave their
Country and Relations to which they
are particularly attached, and under
whofe Conftitution they might expect
fome Protection, to go to a Country
where they could have no fuch profpect.----At no time have the Englifh
been inclined to *emigrate* from their
antient Home---They have not ran to
Scotland, though the latter have to
England---Yet if any thing could induce an induftrious People to wander
from Home, Scotland affords many In-
ducements---She abounds in Fuel---Her
Laws are fimple and ftrictly enforced,
and her People are honeft and well-
informed. There are none of thofe In-
ducements in Ireland.

It has alfo been fancied (and mere
Conjectures fhould prove no Reafon
for the Surrender of fubftantial Acquifitions)

litions) that by a Union, of which the principal Features are a Lofs of Ireland's Parliament, and a *draining* Power repofed in the Hands of a Minifter; the *Spirit* of *Rebellion* would be crafhed. Surely, Gentlemen, there appears nothing in fuch a *difuniting* Meafure, that could tend to produce fuch an Effect; if it fhould appear not to be already filenced for ever.---The gallant Yeomen in Arms, aided by the native Troops of Ireland; have put down the late Rebellion, and with the Affiftance of Providence will again, if ever it fhould rear its *Briftly-head*---The Authors of it have paid feverely for their criminal Audacity and Folly---their Followers have, no doubt, feen their Error, and we may, in their name, fay with Milton---" Thrice happy if they know " their Happinefs and perfevere up- " right"---But fhould there be any

                    amongft

amongſt them ſo fooliſh as to wiſh for
a Republic, in order to pull to Pieces
ſo glorious a Fabric as their Conſtitu-
tion---If there be any *who wiſh* to make
thoſe Wounds (ſo happily inclined to
heal) bleed afreſh, let them, I befeech,
lcok into the Hiſtory of the Civil-
Wars in the Time of Charles the Firſt
and after, ſo fully deſcribed by the
great Clarendon, at the concluſion of
his Hiſtory in the Words following :---
" In this wonderful Manner and with
" this incredible Expedition did GOD
" put an End to a Rebellion that had
" raged near *twenty Years*, and been
" carried on with all the horrid Cir-
" cumſtances of Murder, Devaſtation
" and Parricide, that Fire and Sword,
" in the Hands of the moſt wicked
" Men in the World could be Inſtru-
" ments of; almoſt to the Deſolation
" of two Kingdoms, and the exceed-
" ing

" ing defacing and deforming the " third;"---to which, as to the Irifh Rebellion, we may add the following Words of the fame Author as applicable to the Year 1798 :---" So ended the " Year 1648, a Year of Reproach and " Infamy above all others which had " paffed before it; a Year of the higheft " Diffimulation and Hypocrify of the " deepeft Villainy and moft bloody " Treafons that any Nation was ever " curfed with or under."

As to religious Controverfy it can prove nothing tending to the neceffity of a *Relinquifhment* of parliamentary and other Rights; for it is entirely done away by the Introduction of Irreligion, and the Deftruction of Papal Influence, which has been declining for many Years and received its *final* Death-wound in France, there affailed by the

Hands

Hands of its Followers.---Thus the Root is gone, and the Branches muft follow of courfe---So that if a rebellious Spirit exifts with any in Ireland, it muft be traced to fome, *other* Source, not to be done away by a Union. The example of *licentious France* is the true Fountain-fpring of Rebellion againft the Government.---To *plunder*, and in order to accomplifh that End, to *murder*, have been the criminal objects of the late Rebellion.----To fupport the Conftitution is the only mode of preferving *true Religion*, the Want of which has been the Caufe of many Mifchiefs.---There is no Calamity that ftands more in need of a Cure:----It is in Truth a peculiar Calamity, fallen moft heavily on this Age, which, while it takes its Rife from the Corruption of thofe Times, and has monftroufly increafed fince the *French Revolution* amongft

amongft a certain *Party*, has produced a bare-faced Contempt and Difufe of all Religion whatfoever, fave fome fmall outward Appearance.---With thofe even the Shadow of Godlinefs and Virtue is fled---Atheifm and Prophanenefs, diligently cultivated, have not failed to produce a Proftitution of *all* Manners in Contempt of *all* Governments.

This it is, that may be productive of Difturbances in Ireland; but fuch may very reafonably be expected to meet a fimilar Fate with thofe lately fuppreffed by a gallant and loyal Yeomanry and Soldiery.

Say not, Ye therefore, who vaunt of the Meafure, that Scotland, or any other Country upon the face of the Globe, can be held forth as a *Proof* of the Expediency of a Union with England

I   and

and Ireland; for as each differ, in Point of *Time* and *Place*, there can be no Similarity.

Say not, that by a Union they would confolidate their prefent Legiflatures into one, for their prefent *checking* Power then coming to be loft, all *legiflative Effence* would vanifh.

Say not, that *Articles* of Union would avail, for they could either *directly* or *indirectly* (no matter which) be fwerved from, at any Time.

Say not, that the Power of the Crown would acquire no *preponderating* Weight through a Union, for the *Liberality* of the People of England would not then be *folicited*.

Say not, that Juftice would then be *fairly* and *freely* adminiftered to Ireland, for her *Judges in the laft Refort*, namely,

her

her Peers, would become merged and out of reach, and thus Juftice be un-attainable!

Say not, that by a Union, Irifh Ma-nufacture and Commerce would be ad-vanced, for no Man would, then, lay out his Capital on fo *precarious* a Te-nure!

Say not, that *Englifh* Capital would *flow in*, while *Irifh* flowed out, for as the Englifh have never *flocked* to Scot-land abounding in every Inducement, they would not *flock* to a Country, where their *Winnings* would be plucked from them, at the *Nod* of a Minifter, while ftill they are untrained to wan-dering.

Say not, that the Strength of Eng-land would remain undiminifhed, for

by

by a Depreffion of Wealth you would take from Strength.

Say not, that the Spirit of Induftry in Ireland would not be leffened, for you would deprive the People of the greateft Spur to Induftry, by *fhutting the Doors* of Parliament againft the *moft* ufeful Members of the Community.

Say not, that Abfentees would be beneficial to Ireland, for her quondam Reprefentatives with their Followers alone, would carry 1,000,000, annually out of the Country!

Say not, that Rebellion or fancied Difputes of Religion, can furnifh any juft Pretence for a Union, for the gallant Sons of Ireland have, and at all Times will, ftand forth to quell it.

Say

Say not, that it is neceffary to
ftrengthen, in this Way, the *Hands* of
the Empire; for while acting with
Heart and *Hand*, England has a moft
powerful Support in the Yeomanry
Troops of Ireland, and in the volun-
tary Contributions of her People at
large.

Say not, that if the Irifh Catholics
are as *three* to *one*, they are therefore a
dangerous Body in Rebellion, for it
does not appear, that a Union would
quiet them, the ill-affected of that Per-
fuafion being merely of the *lower* Or-
ders, and urged by *Republican* Principles, as fully proved by their Leau-
ers being principally Democratic Pro-
teftants.

Say not, that it is merely the Gentlemen of the Bar object, because they

as

as being Men of liberal Education, are *well qualified,* and *juftly* relied upon, for their *unbiaffed* Opinions on fo difficult and extenfive a Subject.

Say not, that any Man's *Dictum* fhould ftand in favour of a UNION, for it is the felf-evident Expediency of the Meafure that fhould alone have Weight.

Say not, that Land in Ireland would retain its Value, for a UNION by producing a Decreafe of Wealth, and general Infecurity of Property, the Value of Land muft neceffarily be diminifhed.

But *rather* Say, that England would not be willing to furrender, on fuch an Occafion, *her Public* and *Private* Rights!

Rights!---And *why*, in the Name of *Reafon* fhould *Ireland?*

Ceafe then, Ye declaimers, in Favour of a Meafure, that you muft fee, whilft you have *ftudioufly* avoided touching upon the Subject of *Taxation*, would plunge both Countries into an Abyfs of Mifery!

I now have the HONOR to Subfcribe

myfelf, GENTLEMEN,

Your very obedient,

Humble Servant,

Dublin,
15th Dec. 1798.

E R R A T A.

Page, 7, Read *next* as to her Situation.

9, Read fubfifting *Right of* Reprefentation.

14, Read in feeming favor *of.*

16, Read as that grand Object *can have nothing in View, but* an unbounded.

17, Read having *premifed.*

27, Read the Torrent of Britifh *Weight.*

30, Read there *could* be no Room.

Do. Read crafty Defigns of *any.*

31, Read *and be* fevered.

32, Read in *Oppofition* to the Legiflative.

36, Read and *this* while fhe has.

39, Read *Auguis* for *Anginis.*

Do. Read *muft* be confidered as a mere Delufion.

www.ingramcontent.com/pod-product-compliance
Lightning Source LLC
Chambersburg PA
CBHW030022030726
47499CB00008B/3086